JAMES ALEXANDER COGHLA in 1972. He was rais Initially educated at same school Alexander Fleming, the inventor of Penicillin, attended years ago, James later studied at the Universities of Kingston and Glasgow for his B.A. (Hons.) and M.Litt. degrees. A poet, novelist and a short story writer, James has presented his research papers in Turkey, Poland and Scotland. James now lives in Alloway, Ayrshire. His interests include hillwalking and the protection of the environment.

THE IMPOSSIBLE JOURNEY

A NOVELLA

JAMES A. COGHLAN

ROMAN *Books*
www.romanbooks.co.in

ISBN 978-81-906788-1-0 (Paperback)
ISBN 978-81-906788-2-7 (E-book)

Major Typesetting in Bookman Old Style

First published in January 2009

ROMAN *Books*
2nd Floor, 38/3, Andul Road,
Howrah 711109, WB, India.
www.romanbooks.co.in

British Library Cataloguing in Publication Data.
A catalogue record for this book is
available from the British Library.

Printed and bound in India by
Roman Printers Private Limited.
www.romanprinters.com

In memory of a true Scot –
John William Ford Coghlan

THE IMPOSSIBLE JOURNEY

"External freedom will always be the means of measuring the freedom of the self within."

Mahatma Gandhi

Prologue

'Bugger off then and get yersel killed, ya selfish wee bastard.' She hung out the 3rd storey window of our tenement block in Queen Street, (later to be named, Neptune Street, Govan) and cursed me. 'Yer an ungrateful wee bastard.' Those were the last words my mother said to me. I was only seventeen, but glad to be leaving home.

My older brother Charlie, stopped me on his way back from his engineering job on the Underground. He asked why our mother was shouting. I told him. He shook his head, laughed and said he'd go see his mate Tam Niven. After that he'd go home.

'She'll have calmed doon a bit by then.' Charlie nodded up at our mother. Her face was the same colour as when she got too much sun. There was no way she'd hear him, so Charlie could say whatever he liked, when he did get home.

'Mind an no get yersel killed, Jackie. An say goodbye to the old man. Ye ken he'll miss ye tae.' My family and friends called me, Jackie.

I replied, 'I'll drap ye a line, once I'm billeted. I'll write tae Granny Fitzgerald.'

'Mind and dae that, Jackie. Ye need tae ken how the Gers are playin.'

'I will. See ya, Charlie. An make sure ye dae tell me.'

'I'll be huvin yer winter jaiket.'

'Fine.'

'An I'll also huv yer . . .'

I had walked too far down the street to the Clyde docks and couldn't hear what else he was going to take from my personal belongings. Although in a tenement of that size and with so many people, nothing was ever really your own. And I reckon that's a good thing. It teaches you to share.

Govan never seemed so alive before. I noticed paint on walls of companies that had gone as I walked along the streets. I was excited to be joining their ranks.

I found my father sitting in his usual seat in his wooden hut. He was sad to see me going.

'I'll miss ye Jackie, lad. But, I'll no hold ye back.' He smiled.

A small man, he works harder all his days than men of twice his build. He gave me six shillings. Turning away, to drink a cup of tea, he says, 'Make it last, John.' My father never calls me by my real Christian name. Like my brothers he calls me Jackie. It is a profound moment. One of those moments that you remember to the day you die.

My father has spent his entire life working hard, but never saw any profit for it. His only salvations were that we lived so close to The Red Lion pub and Ibrox. Standing there, I felt a huge flood of pity for him. His cap was flat on his head and he had a tooth missing from his lower left jaw. Instead of joining my father and my brothers Robert, James and Chris at the docks, or Charlie at the Underground, I signed up with the Army.

The Army was good back then. No real questions asked about papers. I took my older brother Chris's papers and only admitted to who I really was when I turned twenty-one in India. There were no real consequences. The RSM only said, 'Ye've made your bed, rifleman. Get on wi it.' Maybe that's what had annoyed 'Big' Maggie as she stood there with her pinnie on and her arms crossed, swearing out the window. She no longer had control of me and my money. Six wages were now five. But as I was only a lad, I still had a lot to learn about the world. India would change all that.

∞

Almost finished Basic Training, when I stumble upon 'the latest in Searchlight technology.' Far be it for me to point out the obvious, but one direct hit from a bullet will render the vehicles' light useless. The tracks on it are meant to improve the performance of the vehicle. How well that works in a bog or deep mud I don't know. Major Jeremy Dalton, one of the older Officers insists that a horse, rider and lamp would be far more reliable.

∞

After Basic Training is complete with the 1st Battalion, Cameronians (Scottish Rifles), I am stationed to Edinburgh Castle. On our first day, me and Campbell end up kidding about killing each other with our rifles and bayonets.

Campbell says, 'Ah'm no' going fur yer throat, Coghlan. Ah'm gonnae kill yer jeely piece. Cos a bugger kens folk fae Glesgae cannae dae wi oot their piece.'

I laugh, 'Aye, well, better n bein a butter boy.'

'Butter boy?'

'Aye, wan o thae boys wha slips up.'

The views of Edinburgh are great, but none more so than from the Castle. It has a great history and we all like it here. There are rumours of ghosts, but I've never met any. Although on a Saturday night, after a few of the boys have been drinking, it looks like we might have the living dead in our ranks. By Monday the truth is known.

After three years of relative quiet in Edinburgh, we travel overnight by train to London. An uneventful six months tour in Gibraltar, before we set sail for India.

I'm not worried by the darkness, nor by the bad weather. I'm too excited to sleep and walk the deck for most of the night. The only place I can sleep is in the engine room. The engineers don't talk to those on deck much, but when I tell them my brother is an engineer, they become friendlier. It's like there are two levels onboard. Those above deck and those below.

ର

After weeks of visiting various ports, we arrive at Calcutta. We catch a troop train to Bombay. The train ride through the heart of India is as breathtaking as the views we witnessed on our travels to India. It feels as if we are returning to Edinburgh. Due to the heat we know this is impossible. I cannot capture any of the scenes I want to as my camera is buried safely inside my spare uniform at the bottom of my kit bag. I cannot get hold of another camera easily and do not want the lens smashed. I write my notes on bits of brown paper-bags.

The cramped conditions in the train remind me of the room and kitchen I share with my family. Soldiers are standing in the corridor of the train, just in order to be able to travel further up the line. It's funny when you are pinned into a corner and have no way of moving unless someone needs to go for a drink or something else. I thought signing up would give me more freedom. I never thought I would have less.

Boats and trains bring us only so far. We finish our journey to Lucknow on foot. Our Regiment arrives at Lucknow, a day late. Our new Commanding Officer (C.O.), Major General Stevenson is unimpressed with our Regiment. Campbell doesn't think much of him and his moustache either.

ॐ

The March past at Lucknow. Marching beats being stuck on boats or trains. It gives the legs a chance to be free. Discipline in our ranks is no problem as all our boys get on well. Even if we do wind up the Officers a bit too much, most of us are decent.

It's no surprise to me when I discover that most of the boys are from Glasgow. After Inspection we see the Barracks. I've seen 'karts' made of tougher stuff. I've made 'karts' of tougher stuff. The latrines are to be dug tomorrow. Some of us are going to help engineering with bridge construction. It seems that one or two of their boys have yellow fever.

&

Ten of us are tasked with building a bridge into the new camp. We have been told that Sergeant Major Bell is hopeful of seeing the bridge complete for parade in the morning. It's a hot afternoon, although there is a little cloud before dinner. Our Officer, Lieutenant Black, abandons us in order to talk to some other officers of the Cavalry about a game of Polo. Rifleman Green and Corporal MacIntosh disappear for an hour without explanation. Campbell and the rest of us in the Engineering unit are hard pressed to complete the bridge on schedule.

What a great sense of accomplishment when we finally finish the bridge! It's unlike other tasks. I enjoy moving the timber around in groups. It's challenging, but I love a challenge. I personally hate digging latrines and welcome the construction of the bridge. However, I gain a dozen splinters. After we eat in the Mess Hall, I spend the rest of the night pulling bits of wood out of my fingers with my teeth.

We have taken only a day to construct a decent footbridge. Angus, a Highlander (grandparents from Shettleston, Glasgow) is our resident engineer. I met him during Basic Training and thought he was First Class. He's handy with his fists and not the type I'd like to cross in a hurry, if at all. He does not talk much, but when he does, it is from the heart. He thinks Campbell is a bit of a chancer.

Campbell thought of getting a couple of elephants to shift the timber. We saw the elephants shifting huge logs on our way into camp. Green and MacIntosh return after they are grilled by Lieutenant Black. He finds the rest of us sweating in the sun. No answer was given by either one of them as to where they were. The two deserters are immediately put on kitchen duties.

ॐ

Having secured the bridge with chains and without the help of elephants, we take a rest to record our valiant efforts. Micky and Huw were taking bets as to when we would complete the structure. Davy McPherson wins with the closest time of 3.50 p.m. When our bridge is inspected, we do not receive any compliments from our Lieutenant—Colin Black. He simply says, 'It'll do, men.' Like many Officers I have come across, he is a man of few words and even tighter with his praise.

Back in barracks, Green and MacIntosh produce some tea and biscuits that they 'liberated from the Officers' Mess with the help of a coolie.' It's not that we do not get food. We are well fed, but in a parallel of the social system in India, our lot is not as good as it could be.

ॐ

Lieutenant Black is currently disciplining MacIntosh, having discovered the irregularities of our bridge-building exercise. One of the other Officers saw Green and MacIntosh head for the

Officers' Mess. Green waited outside and MacIntosh entered alone. In the Mess a coolie was sweeping the floor. MacIntosh slipped him a few rupees and the coolie went out for some fresh air. So, MacIntosh is going to pay back the Officers Mess for the goods he stole. Three shillings.

Green asks the boys to help MacIntosh with 'his debt or he'll no be up fir a drink or cards onie time soon.' We all agree. Campbell takes the three shillings 'donation' to Black himself. Campbell tells Black that we won't see one of our own (MacIntosh), lose out for a moment of stupidity. When Campbell is about to leave Black asks, 'Did ye enjoy the biscuits as much as the tea, Campbell?'

'Nah, bit tae dry fur me, sir.'

'Well, that'll be an end to the matter, Rifleman. No repeats, I hope.'

'Wi they biscuits? Nae chance o that, sir.'

❀

Patrolling the hills near Lucknow is something I enjoy. It reminds me of the Campsies near Glasgow. Huw and Jimmy want to climb the mountains in the Himalaya. They say they have a bet with the Greys that we will be the first to climb that region. I'm all for it. I have no idea where the Himalaya is but the boys don't seem to mind, seeing as I have walked hills since I was a boy. They tell me that they just need one more for their team of six and then we can plan it. We ask around camp, but few are willing to sacrifice their leave to climb hills.

Having marched up and down the Sarju and Pindar valleys, I am quite certain I could go from Govan Cross to Glasgow Green in half an hour. I keep thinking of how everybody is doing back home. I don't beat myself up about it, but find myself keeping notes of funny things for my letters to Charlie. For instance, yesterday when Huw was making tea on patrol, he accidentally put salt into the can instead of sugar. I was the only one to notice. I told the boys not to drink their tea, but they thought I was having a laugh. Then they tasted it themselves. The spray from their mouths soaked Jimmy and myself.

Back at camp, I receive a letter from Charlie. He's only a year older than me. He says Rangers drew with Celtic on Saturday. The letter is a month old. He says the referee missed several hacks. Tam Niven, (Charlie's best mate), says on one occasion the referee should have given a penalty. Robert is still reading and studying—still being plagued by the girls as well. James is doing well at work, but now lives with our grandmother, Ellen. As usual, Charlie ends the letter, 'Take care of yersel, Jackie.' It's late and its been a long hot day, so I will write a reply tomorrow.

છ

Today, we celebrate Empire Day and our regiment forms the word, 'Empire' out of respect for the King. After marching off the ground, we sing to the King, give three cheers and pray. It is a spectacular sight, witnessed by the local Girls' school and the Officers' wives. It gives us some sense of home. A sense of something other than the daily ritual of patrols. A couple of the lads are talking about forming a water polo team. They ask me to join them because I'm a strong swimmer.

The rest of my regiment found out how strong a swimmer I was when our pontoon was caught in a strong current and the anchor rope broke. I jumped off, rope in hand and headed for the shore. The rivers around here are shallow compared to the parts of the Clyde I have endured at the hands of my brothers.

I sent off my letter to Charlie. I told him about the new recruit who dressed up like a Brigadier in order to embarrass Captain Kennedy. Kennedy, it seems, left a young lady in the family way before heading out here. Kennedy has also given the new recruit, Rifleman Rory McPherson a hard time since his arrival. It took Kennedy half an hour to realize it was not really an irate Brigadier seeking assurances from a future son-in-law. The Regiment will never let Kennedy forget it.

Angus was laughing for ages. The tears were streaming down his face at the sight of Kennedy's realization of the truth. Kennedy attempted to discipline Big Angus. I don't think Angus even heard Kennedy speak. My brothers and I are a sort of Regiment, even if a somewhat disheveled lot at that.

After four years, having 'served well' in the North-West Frontier, we move to Delhi. The term is in brackets as it is the only compliment our C.O. has ever given us as a regiment. Once more, upon arrival, we have a march past. This year (1936), we have one of the best water polo championship teams. I am asked to join the local lodge and am happy to accept.

There are many tensions throughout India calling for Independence. There have been street battles in areas where different cultures pray side by side. It reminds me of the situations back home between the Protestants and Catholics of Glasgow when they have street fights. I guess folks across the Empire just like things their own way, whether it's in Delhi or Dundee.

Campbell was sent home last year having fallen to the fevers. I'm not surprised going by the mosquitoes and flies. Our patrols increased for a few weeks due to a wee bit of civil disturbance. It was only after this that we had a week's leave. Campbell left the rest of us to go away with his girlfriend to some hotel. He ended up in the river, having tried it on with the young lady and being refused. Reports say that she was as shocked as he was when he hit the water. One of the Officers fished him out the water and heard her say to Campbell, 'Certain young ladies don't do that sort of thing.'

A few months later Campbell started sweating

at night and coughing during the day. On patrol he was always sweating and tired. Eventually, Angus helped me carry him to see the camp doctor. According to the newspaper Campbell gave me before returning home, Jesse Owens has upset Adolf Hitler by winning an Olympic race against Aryan Germans.

ॐ

For as long as I live, I doubt I will ever know such a life again. As I said to Sergeant Major Bell, in the field hospital in Calcutta (1938), there was nothing I was afraid of more than my mother. Her wish for me to die almost came true. I was in hospital recovering from an injury sustained during operations. However, I was made of harder stuff than to let a metal plate in my right forearm hold me back. It was true that I could no longer hold a rifle at the correct angle, but just when I thought all was lost, the Sergeant Major happened to come across my photographs.

There and then, he asks me if I want to stay in active service. I ask, 'How, sir?' His response is non-committal, but his firm handshake and hand upon my shoulder reassure me. So, it comes about rather than return to my family in Govan, I keep my metal and stay in India. I change from being a rifleman to a photographer.

Intelligence is my new expertise. Had they asked 'Big' Maggie, she'd have died laughing. She said my head was thicker than two planks. She often said, 'Guid for nuthin that wan.' Yet, the Sergeant Major in both build and voice was far bigger by volume. It also turned out that he was to be a better judge of character.

৳৩

Sergeant Major Bell convinces me to join Operation Odessa. Briefly, six of us will drive from Rawalpindi to London posing as tourists, carrying classified cargo. We are not told any more during our briefing in the Mess hall. I have a letter from Charlie saying Hitler has invaded Poland. Everyone thought Chamberlain had secured an honourable settlement with him to avoid war. How wrong we were!

Angus wants to crush the Hun with his bare hands, when he hears the news. He insists they cannot be trusted. Then he tells us, his father fought them in France. Reckons if we can defeat them once, we can do it again. So, we are off tomorrow morning, with our Indian and British papers on our mission to London. We have been told it is too dangerous for us to travel by boat. We must drive to London.

Clem is our Intelligence Officer. He's very much a thinker, royalist and servant of His Majesty. (I have only ever met him twice—once at a Battalion marching competition and once in a dancehall where he was entertaining a quiet but independent young woman.) The young woman returned to England the following day.

Two sets of papers have been organized for our mission. Our Indian papers are in our pockets, our British papers hidden behind the spare wheel of the 2nd automobile. Clem instructs us to enjoy our last night in camp. He insists it'll be a long drive to London. I feel just as excited as I did when I first arrived in India.

 co

What a send off! Angus, Clem, Huw, Jimmy, Micky and I are surprised with the attention we get. Mahmood, one of the coolies, informed Corporal Chapman of our intentions to slip off quietly without any fuss. Chapman being the loud type, decided to get the boys. No doubt, the send off was organized with the help of a few of the Officers. What a spread of food!

We were all told to go to the Mess hall as Sergeant Major Bell had sent for us. Chapman led us in. Then the boys started cheering as we walked into the hall. The songs were great and Sergeant McConnell played his guitar, while one of the Officers' wives thumped religiously on an antiquated piano. At the end of the night, Angus said that we were all grateful for the chance to say goodbye. Having travelled back across India to Calcutta, we six know we must return to the North-West Frontier and begin our journey at Rawalpindi. It is there we shall collect our classified cargo.

I have sent another letter to my brother Charlie. He writes to me every month, with the latest football scores. If he is too ill, he tells one of my other brothers, Robert, James or Chris to write to me. Though each of them only wrote to me once in his absence.

'Big' Maggie, it seems, does not talk about me to the neighbours. She doesn't know where I am. I send my letters to Charlie via Ellen Fitzgerald, (my grandmother), who lives at 26d Copland Road. She has not spoken to our mother since they had an argument nine years ago. I could never work out why they fell out. I only remember the row was something about a porcelain teapot with the King on it. I am tempted to send 'Big' Maggie tea in a tin, but I doubt she'd find it funny. On the other hand, my brothers would be in stitches for days.

ʬ

Day 1

Leaving Rawalpindi. We are given an escort as far as Taxila by two armoured automobiles. Out of the back of our automobile, I can see the local boys walking behind us. It is a fantastic gesture and one that we all appreciate. We pull in to let them pass us. They will lead us, until it is time for them to return to camp.

'You boys are lucky tae be ridin hame,' Corporal Chisholm says as I sit in the back of the 2nd automobile.

'Ur we?,' I reply.

'Aye, freedom an the open air. No stuck in a tin can oot at sea.'

'Ye'r richt aboot that,' I reply.

'Wish Ah was goin. . . . Got onie room?'

'No. Not this time, Corporal.' Clem ends the conversation quickly and looks at me with questioning eyes. Later, I realize he wants to know what I said, but I simply reassure him that nothing of importance was discussed.

ॐ

Just before Hasan Abdal we meet our next escort. It seems that for a little while we are the local heroes. It is nice to know that we will not have to worry about being shot at for the foreseeable future. At least, we know that if we are shot at by rebels, we will have more than our five rifles and pistol to shoot back.

Operations in India are usually calm affairs, with very little trouble from any armed rebels. Occasionally the locals riot, but then I've been to many a football game at New Year. And these games have riots caused by the referee giving a penalty to the other team. During the riots in India, General Medcalf usually has us patrolling for hours. All our energies are spent to no real end. The uprising normally collapses within a few days and judging by the lack of troops on the ground it is more due to the good spirits of the locals than any tactical advantage we may have displayed. When General Medcalf retires, his replacement General

Collington has a far different approach. He does not believe in wasting resources chasing ghosts. Instead, he would wait until the riots are at their peak and then he would intervene. Until then, the locals can burn off as much energy as they want. Collington's approach is cast iron.

General Collington was Bell's prodigy. I was unaware of it at the time. I have since learnt that it was Collington who noted my passion for photography. Apparently, Collington shares the same passion. Yet, we never spoke face to face, except on one occasion when I was delivering a message to the Sergeant Major. Even then I only managed to say, 'Nice morning, General.'

'Indeed it is, Rifleman,' he replied gazing across the parade ground.

ॐ

We stop for lunch. Naan bread and rice with a bit of meat. While Huw is walking around the front of the first vehicle, he notices a snake charmer under a tree fifty yards up the road. Unlike us, the locals are protected from the heat of the sun by its large canopy. Underneath the tree the breeze keeps us all cool.

Sanjay Marwah has never been bitten in his forty years as a snake charmer. Kader and Rajiv, his two sons, are keen to learn from their father. The boys say, 'father is famous as the only man to wrestle adult Python.' Throughout the region, the six of us are entertained by such sights and fantastical stories.

Clem takes roll call after we set up camp. After ticking off our names he announces, 'I don't see the point in this. It's not as if you lot are deserters.' He never takes roll call again for the rest of the journey.

৪৩

Day 2

Having come across nothing of interest strategically placed to photograph, Angus says maybe I should give a traffic report to HQ. So, I record two trucks in a crash. Angus says, in his rather humorous tone, 'Then the buggers cannae say ye've been at it, Jackie. If they think ye've been on yer arse the damn trip, ye'll end up behin a desk, lad. Ah'm no fur it masel.'

And come to think of it, neither am I. So, if the only thing of interest is where we cross a bridge or where we drive then that's what they'll get. I'm a bit suspicious of it all, but then as they say, 'Ye can take the man oot o Govan, but ye cannae take Govan oot the man.' Clem laughs when I say this.

The two truck drivers have been arguing for ten minutes. They both insist that the other is to blame for the crash. Clem asks them which of them was in the truck on the inside. Yassim gives a big grin and says that he was indeed respectful of the road and that he was in the truck. Clem asks him

30

why he was so close to the inside of the road. Yassim says that he did not want to drive off the edge of the road by accident. Farooq, the second driver, heading in the same direction as we are, asks how he is to deliver goats that are injured.

Clem suggests that the injured goats are killed and then sold to the tribal people of the region. So, we are now heading North again, having helped move the truck with a broken front axel. The two drivers are in the other truck with the goats and are now talking as if they are brothers. Clem asks me what I think of it all.

I reply, 'Ah'm just glad we're on oor way again. I thought fir a minute we might huv tae go back.'

Clem replies, 'If I have to carry you all over the mountains on my back like a coolie, then I will.'

Micky then says, 'Why wait, Clem?'

જી

Peshawar. I ask for a photograph and am pleased when Markhor, his son Sharpu and Abdulla and his son, also called Sharpu, agree to pose for one on the steps of a local business. It only costs me twenty rupees. Markhor is 45, seated on the top left and his son Sharpu is 23. Abdulla seated on the top right does not know how old he is. His son is 24.

We are asked if we want to buy trophies. Kashmir goats and various other animal furs are put before us. It's not strange to see hunting trophies are prized as far North as this. India is a country of many cultures and climates and I find it particularly funny that the world over, people are actually the same. I think of my brothers and then take another photograph. We do not stay long in Peshawar and head for the border before sunset.

ॐ

Day 3

The last checkpoint before the border with Afghanistan convinces us we are getting further and further from camp. The hills are covered in snow. Our Punjabi comes in slightly useful as we share a drink of tea with the Indian soldiers stationed here.

'Normal rules do not apply up here, boys,' Clem says. He is intent on leaving a positive picture of us with all our acquaintances and gives our hosts a gift—a tin of tea. After the sun sets outside and we have only candles to see by, he encourages the rest of us to enjoy our last night in India. (I now realize Clem foresaw dangers that I could only imagine. Although, he was only four years my senior, he always came across as an old man. But those who only saw that side to him, never truly knew nor liked the heart of the man.)

Heavy snow during the night. Micky, Jimmy and I are too cold to sleep. We start playing cards and are soon joined by the others. We decide to leave early. Our hosts see us off. We don't wave or say goodbye. They know we'll never talk again. We are unsure when we will next sleep in a building. Clem reckons we will reach Kabul before supper, unless the road ahead is blocked by snow. The one good thing about being back at barracks was regular mealtimes. Out here, well, we eat when we can.

ಇಂ

Day 4

We have been told that the Khyber Pass is blocked and we cannot get through to Kabul. The crew of the TRAFALGAR tell us not to drink the snow as it will burn our lips. The coolies have given them this sound advice. Instead, they tell us to put it in our canteens, between us on the seats of our automobiles. They tell us to let it melt naturally. After an hour, we can drink it safely. We are used to the metallic taste, but not the purity of the water.

The Khyber Pass is indeed blocked by snow. Fortunately, a few of the coolies help us. After eight hours of shovelling and digging, we break through. What a site it is! What a celebration! We have conquered again, beaten back nature!

The cold has gone for our fingers and faces. I cannot feel my fingertips in either hand. My feet are numb. The rest of the lads are freezing too. Angus seems immune to it all. Jimmy is convinced that somebody back at HQ is having a laugh at our expense.

Our helpers are unhappy that the driver of the truck behind is thumping his horn. Huw stops Angus from burying the driver in the deep snow. I understand the driver's frustration. Most likely, he has been cramped in that truck of his for hours on end.

The driver shouts an insult to the coolies who answer in chorus that he could not go anywhere as there was no way through. The Khyber Pass at this point is only nine feet across. Angus tells him to take his hand off the horn or he'll find his truck down at the bottom of the Peshawar valley. The driver gets out and watches us all continue to dig the road clear. Micky keeps a friendly hand on Angus.

Temperatures are very close to freezing all day. The thermometer says that it is two below already and it's only 10 p.m. Abul Fazl, the local tribal leader, tells us that travellers do not come this way during the winter because of the heavy snowfalls. He says more than that and warns us against continuing on our journey. After only four days, we are keen to push on into Afghanistan. We will make the border by morning. For the moment, we six are in a small shack with four of our hosts. We offer two hundred Rupees for our food and lodging, but our hosts start to push us out into the snow. We apologize, not meaning to offend. After a few drinks, we head to our makeshift beds. Animal furs on the floor of a hut are better than the seats in our vehicles.

We have all begun to dislike the confined space that an automobile affords us. It is really good to have an excuse to stop rather than be stuck in our seats for hours at a time. I feel that only if you have driven a delivery truck or automobile for days will you truly appreciate the freedom of the open air, especially those first few steps when the blood gets back into your legs. I miss being on patrol.

Sure, sometimes we had to walk for miles, but it gave you a chance to really see things. I feel like we are missing so much as we drive past the villages and people on our mission to London.

ೞ

Day 5

The last tunnel in India. We are almost at the border of Afghanistan. It's a strange feeling. I have been in India for seven years. Now I am sad to be leaving. Although, I did not come alone and will not leave alone, I still feel a sense of loss. It's as if the road on the other side of the tunnel is filled with dangers I can sense. I do not think this beautiful country of India or I will ever be the same again. We drive for another hour and then stop for dinner, before setting up camp.

Setting up camp is a routine affair that we soldiers are used to. Huw and Angus, being the tallest in the group, work as a unit within our company. Jimmy secures the ropes and Micky collects wood while Clem and I organize dinner. It's very much like a tourist holiday, despite the daily reminders to the contrary.

After dinner we usually discuss the next day's drive and then sit and talk about being back at home. Back home seems so far away when you are miles from any signs of human life. It is as if we have gone backwards in time to a place where men have never been. Clem says it reminds him of a story by H. G. Wells.

∞

Naan bread for lunch. We also have some rice and herbs, but our lot is small and shall last for a few days yet. We each have a responsibility. Jimmy looks after the vehicles. Angus looks after the tents. I take a great joy in monitoring the food. Huw looks after the petrol. Micky looks after the money and papers. Clem looks after the weapons, concealed under the rear seats in each vehicle. We each have a role to play in our mission. It gives us a focus and responsibility. Back at camp, we each had something to do. Our roles have changed, but not the purpose. I'm not supposed to write down names or places. My brief is to take photographs.

We have long discussions about those we consider to be our heroes. When asked, I cannot think of anyone except my father. I rarely went to the cinema and I didn't want to name a footballer as two of the others had done so.

The terrain is harsh here. We are miles from the nearest Battalion HQ. In the distance we see some figures moving. Now that we are so far North and within minutes of the frontier, we are becoming increasingly cautious. The NWF (North-West Frontier) was once crossed by the Romans. I wonder what they thought of it when they came here? I can only imagine they found the region as inhospitable as the reception a penniless drunk gets in a brothel.

After lunch we come across another barrier. The sign on the bridge reads, 'BRIDGE UNSAFE FOR WHEELED TRAFFIC'. A river runs below the bridge. We cannot see a way across nearby and think we might need to drive further north. We have no choice other than to try and find a shallow part of the river as there are no more bridges for twenty miles. Micky and Jimmy are hungry. Angus and Huw are tired of driving. Clem tells Angus to stretch his legs and then take the back seat. Clem is going to drive the second automobile. After all, it is his.

෬

Crossing the river. There are no bridges available to cross. The nearest one is unsafe. It looks like a death trap. We decide to cross at the shallowest point of the river. However, the time delay causes serious problems. The black automobile crosses first. We wait for it to reach the far bank.

The others shout to us from across the river, but the wind drowns out their attempts to help us navigate. Angus, Clem and I are half way across, before we realize that the river is rising rapidly. Angus says we are following the same line as the lead automobile, but I am unconvinced. Clem says that the snow may be melting on the hills and that might explain why we are suddenly being flooded.

Angus and I are told to make a run for it. I realize now that Clem wanted to lighten the load and therefore make the vehicle more buoyant. Turns out that he was in a rowing club, too. I never heard which one. The wind claimed that secret.

So, while Angus and I head for dry ground, Clem stays with the vehicle, convincing her to climb onto a pile of shale that is far too steep for her. Moving her up and down and side to side, he will not quit. He does not want to leave her to the fate of the river. He seems to take it as a personal insult that the river wants to claim the automobile from him. I would later learn that Clem was the type who would *never* leave anyone behind. He considers it bad form. Having being educated at a Boarding School in Edinburgh, he has a very matter of fact way of dealing with very complex issues.

Clem and the second automobile are stranded on an island of rocks. The snow has thawed quicker than we all anticipated. The lower half of our vehicle vanishes right before our eyes. Clem stays in the driver's seat while Angus and I run for help. Thankfully, we just passed a checkpoint. The others were unable to help having reached the far bank ahead of us. They are temporarily trapped on the other side of the river.

We all get soaked in the process. Our trousers are wet above the knee. I'm used to it, but Clem is annoyed. How he stays above water is a miracle to me. I think the engine is going to be flooded. He remains with the automobile and the wooden chest entrusted to our little party. He even manages to keep his hat dry.

There are several jokes about Clem being unsinkable at this point. He shakes his head and produces a talisman from around his neck. He says it is his lucky chain. His girlfriend (Jessica) had given it to him. She had been scared that he would be shot or killed. She made him promise never to take it off. That way she asserted, he could never die. I do not know if Clem believed the talisman made him invulnerable, but he did show us the chain of silver links.

After setting up camp, we spend the evening stripping and drying our weapons. With the aid of a little oil they are soon operational.

Clem insists that we do not drive across any more rivers, even if the weather has been dry. He does not want to risk damaging the cargo. When Huw asks what it is, Clem ignores him and starts talking about the travel plans for the morning. Huw, never one to quit, keeps at Clem. Clem becoming annoyed with Huw, turns suddenly and says,

'It's a box full of hope. Hope that must reach London. Whatever it takes.'

'Right-oh Clem. I was only askin.'

'And I'm only telling.'

'Gie us a peek.'

'I'm not allowed to do that. The chest cannot be opened.'

'How no?'

'Just listen to me. Forget it's even here. Just forget it.'

Realizing Clem is deadly serious going by the glint in his eye, Huw and the rest of us for that matter don't mention the wooden chest again.

Day 6

We cross the Border. We have completed the passage out of India. For me this is a spectacular occasion. Upon my arrival in India, I was determined never to return to Glasgow. It was as if I had been given wings. It was as if someone had carried me far from the chains that bound me. Freedom. Yet, I do miss my friends. Especially Sandy Patterson and Davy Kirkmichael. I miss my brothers too and often wonder what they are doing down at the docks. And I really miss talking to my old man at night.

I would always ask my father about important things. There were a lot of times during my time in India when I wished I could have just talked to him. When Sergeant Major Bell asked me what I wanted, I imagined I could run up the close, into our room and kitchen to ask my old man. I would not ask my mother. (Much later, she was in Clydebank visiting her sister, my Auntie Gwen, when she had been caught short during an air raid. Convinced by the distant thuds that it was safe to venture to the lavatory at the bottom of the garden, 'Big' Maggie made a dash into the darkness. Auntie Gwen actually states she saw the bomb hit the toilet. Bits of newspaper lay across the garden. My mother was never found.)

⠃⠕

I like what the sign says at the Afghan Border; 'It is absolutely forbidden to enter Afghan territory.' It sums it all up. Here is a barrier. What's a barrier for? It's just another fence or wall. And where I am from, you use one or both to outrun the 'Polis' through the tenements.

You can even use walls for climbing onto church roofs and getting hold of lead piping which the scrappy will give you a shilling for. So, my brothers Charlie and Robert tell me. Well, Robert did until he got caught. He was for legging it, but Charlie was stuck on a sharp piece of metal and was scared to rip his trousers.

Charlie knew 'Big' Maggie would give him hell if he ripped his trousers. So, instead they both got a clip round the ear, marched home and beaten with the belt by my mother. The Sergeant knew them both on sight. He had tears in his eyes and was laughing as he described how Charlie looked pinned to the roof.

My mother said they were both going to hell. That was ten years ago. So, when I saw this sign with the word 'FORBIDDEN,' I was determined to enter Afghanistan, in memory of what my two older brothers did not manage to do. Upon returning to Scotland, I will tell them of the sign.

While I am taking the photograph, Clem asks us if we are certain that we still want to carry on. Angus says, 'Listen tae me lad, if ye think Ah'm gonnae turn tail ye can. . . . Orders is orders, sir.'

Clem raises his hand and looks the big man in the face. Then Clem looks at each of us in turn. Realizing our resolve to stay together, regardless of the consequences, Clem says, 'Ok, on to Kabul.'

I do not think he will ever question our loyalty to the mission again. Although, I'm certain he expected the reaction he got. Maybe the real reason he asked us was his conscience. He knew we really are going to be breaking rules and regulations and so he wanted us to decide for ourselves. I'm glad we stood as one. I'll never know what would have happened had one of the others said they wanted to turn back.

ℬ

Afghan Territory. Some tribes use the goat to get rid of sins—the scapegoat. But, there are no scapegoats here. The tribe we are with is descended from the tribe of Benjamin. Yet, today the goat is not to be used to rid anyone of sins, nor is it to be used as the 'ball' in the game of 'Buzkashi' (played only in Afghanistan.) Today, we will have goat curry, a local dish in the region of Kashmir.

Micky insists he's not hungry. When offered the first serving, Clem merely smiles and thanks our hosts. He manages a smile after his first mouthful. Micky excuses himself and we hear him being sick some distance from the tent. Clem explains that Micky has been ill to our hosts and that he has not been eating. I had only just realized that Micky had been a bit under the weather and actually hadn't eaten too much in the last day or so. What Clem was saying to our hosts, wasn't actually a lie.

We celebrate Afghan culture with our hosts and toast their long life. For ourselves, we make private prayers that we will reach London. Huw only tells me his thoughts as he blows out the candle.

ഇ

Day 7

Kabul. My camera is still wet from being caught in the river. I have no option but to let it dry by the fire. It keeps making a screeching sound when I press the button to take a photograph. Jimmy says it just needs some grease and oil. He opens it and performs a bit of engineering surgery on it. I am enthralled while the rest of the boys sit and discuss the next day's driving. We are in a small hotel with three rooms, but for now we are all in Jimmy and Micky's room. The view from their window is of high ridges in the distance.

We let Micky have as much milk as will settle his stomach. It is only as we leave that we discover it is goat's milk. I have really enjoyed India for all its different foods and even beyond it we are trying new things. Although, some of us clearly don't want to eat a plateful of goat. I prefer fish. I'm just thinking of fish and chips when I get back to London.

Day 8

I have had to let my camera and equipment dry since our little adventure in the river three days ago. I have taken one or two photos, but the film is wet and I have to dry it by the camp fire tonight. Jimmy's repairs have had a little impact, but I'm surprised I was able to get it to function at all. So, to pass the time I decide to draw a map of where we are today. It is a very crude map and one that Micky will no doubt improve upon in his own way. Yet, it shows the road we will travel in our hearts and minds, not knowing what new challenge will present itself to us.

Early rise today means we were able to get ahead of our target destination of Tahrud. We have followed the same road for the last two hours without seeing a soul. We stop for lunch and fresh water supplies at Kerman. We discuss how long we are driving today. Normally, we spend twelve hours in our vehicles. Today, we decide on ten. Confidence is high and we agree to push on beyond Yazd. Clem is confident that we will reach London in three weeks. The rest of us will be happy just to reach the next hotel with a warm bath. Clean water from a tap would be good, or even from a water-seller.

The deserts are covered in ruins of bygone moments of celebration and life. We decide to camp in a ruin for the night, reasoning that we will be off the main road and sheltered from the extreme drop in temperature that occurs around four in the morning.

The desert is such a contrast to the tenements of Glasgow or the barracks we have stayed in. Micky says, 'I dinnae mind the quiet, Jackie. I just cannae staun aw the sand in ma food.' After saying that he spits out the last piece of a pie. He lights his clay pipe and walks over to ask Clem something. Micky is the quietest in our little group, but he is the fastest runner and best shot with a rifle.

After setting up camp, Jimmy says he misses the barracks and his bed. He says he even misses the RSM's dulcet tones. Angus and Micky start laughing at this point. Clem just looks at them both sideways. Angus and Micky stop laughing.

The rest of us have noticed that Jimmy is looking increasingly tired. He has come to the conclusion that the desert is no place for sleeping. The cold wakes him and then his neck injury, gained during the Water Polo Championships of '36, starts to ache. Jimmy says he's fine and that it would be best if we leave him alone. We all agree. He did not win the Battalion Boxing Championships for no reason. Even Big Angus won't upset the wee man. And if Jimmy ever gives you that stare, you just walk away slowly.

Day 9

Tehran is a place of quiet prayer. We arrive in the city without any troubles, hearing the call to prayer. The tyres of our vehicles are looking a bit worn. Clem says we will need to change them soon. I realize that the sights and peoples that we have seen, we will never see again. I am thankful for my camera. I know we will not be going back through these places and begin to get a real appreciation for what we are actually doing. I am also grateful that I am not paying for the fuel. It is here, I learn that Clem is the son of an Earl.

જી

Day 10

It's always a very difficult process when you reach a Border fort. You plan ahead, act casual, and really try to be high spirited. You might pretend to be tourists on holiday. We sing in our automobile, while the others remain quiet in theirs. We act different in order to draw attention to ourselves, in order to draw attention away from the others. We have proved that we can negotiate our way through any difficulty, so far.

Clem always separates us, in case things go wrong. He is an admirer of Alexander the Great.

Thinking on your feet is good for us all, he says. He does not like anything to get in the way of our mission, and approaches new situations with caution. So, before we reach each Border fort, we hand out the weapons, ensuring they are concealed, but available. Then we separate by half a mile. To avoid suspicion, we never talk within sight of the Border soldiers. Yet, today feels different. Jimmy says he senses trouble brewing in his water. Angus tells him to go to the toilet.

ॐ

Thank God, Govan and the King! We've just escaped with our lives. None of us are injured. The windows of the other automobile are shot out. But thanks to quick thinking by Clem, we are all still alive.

I have never seen anybody reverse an automobile and shoot at the same time, but thankfully Clem managed both. Clem says that ever since he went hunting with his father at the age of twelve on their Estate in Perthshire, he has been able to shoot from the back of a moving horse. The automobile merely replaced the horse. He made us put black boot polish over the letters of the lead automobile, so that we do not get too much attention.

We are now safely at Ramadi. We decide to find the nearest 2nd Battalion HQ for repairs, new tyres and a stiff drink. Jimmy and Huw are standing at the rear of the Nairn bus. The other automobile is inspected for bullet damage in the middle of the door. Clem pays for the vehicle to be fixed. Whenever he disappears he always comes back with a handful of notes. Micky is convinced Clem prints money.

The lead automobile needs a new windscreen and left door. The left door has a big hole in it. Posing as tourists worked well, until some rebels attempted to stop us after the last Border fort. They asked to search our automobiles at gun point. Huw said that is what caused the argument with the soldiers at the Border fort. Huw said he had explained things away, without a full search and then we had moved on. But, the rebels were not so easily talked out of it.

I'm still trying to put the pieces together. The others were in the automobile ahead. We had only just left the Border fort and could still see it. Angus and Huw were talking to the rebels. Jimmy, Micky and I were waiting at a distance. Then there was a struggle, Clem was driving forward then backwards and balancing his rifle over the side of his door. As we were some distance away, we had to jump out and start shooting. Yet, for all our handiwork, one got away. So, to avoid being followed by a larger group of rebels, we had to chase the one horseman who had dodged our bullets. At this time, the soldiers began to run towards us. They too started shouting and shooting. We managed to escape with our lives and egos intact, but our automobiles were damaged.

Our little engagement brought about a very strange set of events. I later discover that the rebel leader responsible for airing our vehicles is caught by the 2nd battalion after six days of evading them in the desert.

Clem receives a telegram from London telling him that our little 'party' is to avoid Constantinople/Istanbul. France is beginning to look unreachable. Paris is on our route, but London suggests we rethink that too. Clem says the new plan is to head for a little known port called Yaluva, Turkey. In Yaluva, we will meet Captain Afitap who will help us. Clem says nothing more to us. London instructs him:

DO NOT ENGAGE IN HOSTILITIES UNLESS ABSOLUTELY NECESSARY. STOP.

After Clem shows us all the telegram, Angus asks, 'Whit dae that lot think we're aw daein? Shootin bloody rabbits? Did ye no tell them Clem?' Clem nods his head. Angus swears. The rest of us keep out of it.

Travelling in such a small unit teaches you not to get involved. You have to tolerate the snoring in an eight man tent. You have to get used to the humming and whistling in the middle of the desert. There is no option, when you are stuck in the middle of nowhere, but to tolerate it. It teaches you patience, working as a tight unit. You have to cover each other. You have to bond. So, you overlook the annoying habits. Soon, you find strangers know more about you than your own family. Tonight we are staying in a hotel with hot water and a freshly cooked warm meal. It is amazing how much we take for granted, until we cannot get access to it— hot food, decent drinking water and so on.

୨

Day 11

The bus from Damascus to Baghdad. At least, we know we are on the right road. We spent the last three hours sitting on the road as the sand was blown in our faces. Sandstorms are horrible. I thought I had had a varied life. You cannot see where you are going in a sandstorm. You cannot see where you have been. You cannot see how big the storm is and as the wind and sand rips past you, you have no idea how long you will be stuck in that one place.

Thankfully, we heard the Nairn bus before it hit us. I still have no idea how the driver drove through that storm. After that we pressed on behind him. We knew that we might end up in Damascus, but that was a chance we were ready to take. We simply want to reach the next Battalion HQ.

I think I need a new camera. My lens and capture button have not been the same since their dip in the river.

Our Battalion will be sailing to London from Calcutta by now. We have not been told where we will serve next. However, there were rumours in camp before we set off on our journey that it would be Aldershot. I'd prefer to be stationed at the Tower of London. I might then have a chance of finding my brother Charlie who is currently an artillery gunner near there.

Day 12

We have passed Rutba and are near the Junction. Now, we must head North for Damascus, then Istanbul. It's nice to be able to stop and look around instead of moving on all of the time. We eat lunch here. I feel a certain kinship with these people. They are friendly once they realize we mean no harm and the children are inquisitive.

Jimmy, from all appearances, is suffering from dysentery. We will have to take him to see a doctor or to a hospital. He insists he is fine.

Fifteen miles of desert before we have access to petrol. The heat is almost fatal. I drink water for five minutes. I have never been so thirsty in all my life. Although patrols in Calcutta and Delhi can be very warm, nothing has ever made me want water so badly.

Gold is good currency in any place, it seems. Micky plays down his efforts in getting petrol for the white automobile, although we worked together on that long run. Our commitment to the mission was demonstrated, when we enlisted the help of a local businessman to convert our small gold chains into cash. It seems we are not the first travellers to receive the luxury of his services. His brother Hakim owns the garage from where we buy our petrol. Soon we are back in familiar territory.

In an effort to bolster the local British Army resources, the automobiles have been converted to armoured vehicles. The armour is not thick at all. The RSM tells us that nine Brenn tanks are due next week.

Micky, Huw and I agree that we should take two of the armoured vehicles. Clem is opposed to the idea. The scary thing is that I'm only half serious, but know that Huw is deadly serious. Consequently, our enquiries to obtain two of the vehicles only meet with laughter from the Company's Captain. Our black automobile is just outside his office door. Huw is currently outside 'choosing' which two armoured vehicles we will 'borrow'.

Jimmy speaks to the camp doctor and is given something for his dysentery. Shortly after I write the above, gunfire is heard behind the buildings to our right. Then the two rows of armoured vehicles disappear in a storm of dust and our two automobiles are left out in the open. If rebels are nearby, our vehicles have moved from being no threat to being the only targets of interest. Clem decides it is time for us to leave. We set up camp two hours later.

୨୦

Day 13

I have decided to be the nightwatch. So, I ask Clem. He agrees. After our recent encounters near the Border fort in the desert, he says, 'It's a good idea, Jackie.' I start tonight.

Privately, I'm asked if I'm likely to fall asleep. I explain my father is a nightwatchman at the docks in Govan. I say, 'As a lad Ah'd mebbe sit wae him or go on a walk doon the quay.' So, I'm removed from the possibility of arguing with anyone during the day. It also means I don't need to drive for a while. My arm has been bleeding, but I still wanted to do my bit. I've managed to hide the blood from the others, but the flies smell it.

Now, I sleep most of the day in the back seat of the white automobile. The others don't seem to mind. I overhear Angus saying, 'The wee man's got oor backs, Ah tell ye that.' To be honest, I need the rest for a day or two. The pain in my arm gets worse during the day. So, if I can get some sleep it will help.

While the rest of my unit sleeps, I sit in the black automobile parked near our tents. Every hour, I walk in a circle around the perimeter of the tent. Normally, I scout the area before dark and move any objects that could trip me later on my patrol. I count out ten paces, drive a stick into the ground and then take another ten paces and repeat the process. In the dark, these miniature posts help me move around. The sky is normally clear or at most only has a few clouds. So, it's fairly easy to see.

During daylight, I also make a mental note of trees and rocks. I'm also aided on my patrol by the headlights which are left switched on and facing away from the boys. On my return to the automobile, I switch the lights off. The whole exercise, after all precautions have been taken, takes less than three minutes, but it is enough to stir me from any thoughts of sleep. It's also fun to look out on the hills with only the stars for company. I'm aware that out there in the dark there are snakes and scorpions, but they do not move around too much at night.

The heavens are a truly remarkable sight, when you are so used to the gas lamplights of Govan. My granny, Ellen Fitzgerald, says that 'grampa' Fitzgerald used to use the stars to navigate when he was at sea. I wish I knew the names of the Constellations above my head! I know that our little unit is really privileged in doing what we have done and seeing what we have seen and will see.

୫

Day 14

Yaluva, Turkey. Clem is relieved to find Captain Afitap's boat waiting in harbour for our arrival. Turkish born and bred, the Captain's cousin works in some government department in London. Clem only speaks a little Turkish, but manages to convey the change of plans to our new friend. Captain Afitap suggests a bold move. We are to sail up the Danube through Germany. 'It's great. The Hun wud ne'er think o it. Six Scots made up as Indians, on a Turk's boat, sailin the Danube,' Micky shakes his head as he repeats what Clem tells us. Huw and Jimmy look at each other, but say nothing. Angus smiles.

Clem then asks, 'Well, is it any more dangerous than anything we have done so far?' When he puts it like that, we all shake our heads. We have faced chilling temperatures, fevers, desert suns, bullets and dysentery. Sailing through the middle of Germany, in a Turkish boat, does seem a bit quick and easier than driving across a continent at war. So, we all agree to pay Captain Afitap for his troubles. He signals to Clem that if the money that is offered is not promptly put back into someone's pocket, then our automobiles are going into the harbour. As we are currently at the mercy of the good Captain, Clem decides to keep our payment until the end of the journey.

'Well, wee man, you'll no huv tae dae the graveyard shift the nicht,' Micky says.

It is only now I realize he is right. It will be difficult for any one to approach us on our boat without the Captain or his son seeing them.

�✷

Given the dimensions of the boat and the weight of cargo, Huw is worried that we will sink. It takes Captain Afitap an hour to calm him, with the help of Clem, before we can load the second automobile. After two hours we set sail. Huw's back in form telling us about the characters in Cardiff and the pubs we should visit. As we reach the Port of Istanbul, Huw confesses that he cannot swim.

Clem stands at the back of the boat with the wooden chest at his left side. Nobody asks him if he wants them to watch it for him. Like a Master and dog, the two are now inseparable. He truly is devoted to that piece of luggage.

It's true that the boat is not new. Nor have we just used AVON tyres to travel to London, but the outbreak of war has cut short our plans to wander where we would. We had been due leave. A holiday. Imagine a holiday. Rest. No driving. Complete rest.

It could have been a fun trip, like the one to the Himalaya. Yet, ours is now a trip of survival. We know that it is not just the automobile that can be covered in shoe-polish. We cover our faces, necks and hands in tan shoe-polish. Captain Afitap intends to tell any German boarding parties we are Indian and unable to speak German, English or French. This misinformation he hopes will stop anyone examining us too closely, especially if his story is supported by our Indian papers. Although, judging by our encounters to date, we would most likely overcome our foes.

Once we leave port we cover ourselves in the boot polish. I am not disrespecting any of the wise men I have known, but Clem is a big fan of Al Jolson. It is Clem who has the idea of hiding our true identities. We do not carry face-paint and Angus is strongly opposed to the idea, until we get him drunk. Then, he thinks it'd be great fun to 'get one over' on the Hun. We all have to do it, if we are to get along the Danube posing as Indian tourists. I do not voice my concerns. I think that our skins are dark enough anyway from our years served in India. But, I apply the polish anyway.

ॐ

Day 15

Istanbul. Against orders, (there's a surprise), we enter Istanbul. Captain Afitap wants to visit the Blue Mosque for prayers, before we commence the hardest part of our journey. Clem tells him that we are NOT supposed to enter Istanbul, but the Captain points to his Qur'an. We all decide to enjoy the walk around one of the most spectacular cities of the ancient world. Huw and Jimmy want to buy some more supplies. Angus says he wants a new razor. He hates being unshaven for days. Micky wants a newspaper.

The harbour master is inquisitive, but Captain Afitap dissuades him from talking to us. We wait outside while voices are raised inside the harbour master's office. Clem is about to get involved when the Captain's son, Kimsin pulls him back from the door. The young man just shakes his head and motions us away from the building. So, we find ourselves in the gardens beside the Blue Mosque. Huw asks if we can drive to Paris from here. Clem shakes his head and mutters, 'the route is impossible.'

Jimmy swings between Huw and Micky, as if sweeping them away for some Scottish Country Dancing. Angus and I hear Jimmy say, 'Ye might no want tae say tae much Scots there boys.' I agree that the two of them might not want to be heard talking too much English, when they are supposed to be Indian. Jimmy is chewing the inside of his cheek. I think it's not a case of nerves, but one of self-control. He is losing his temper. His face is beetroot and I can see the nerves sticking out in his neck.

The afternoon is one of rest. We are glad to be able to stretch our legs, instead of being stuck inside our automobiles. Angus, unlike the rest of us, is keen to get on. Huw keeps wondering when we will be leaving Istanbul. The rest of us are keen to have a bath and book into the Grand Hotel De Londres for the night. We all have a fresh bath and a shave. Afterwards, the hotel bar surrenders to our invasion. We barter for fresh razors and soap at the Grand Bazaar.

Jimmy is drawing buildings, people, animals and plants. He is more comfortable on foot than in either vehicle. I'm pleased to be in a city where I can photograph buildings instead of fields and hills too. Boredom is the worst part of driving for mile after mile.

It's hard to remember who we are at times. One day we are soldiers, next day tourists, another day Scottish, another day Indian. Jimmy insists we can all get parts in the Music Halls if we're short for a job back home. He loves the Music Halls.

Back aboard our little Turkish boat, Angus says if he hears Glenn Miller's Tuxedo Junction for the 215th time, he will send the gramophone and Jimmy to a watery grave. He's only joking about Jimmy, but not about the gramophone, by the way he is calculating its weight with an unrelenting stare. Micky is sitting quietly looking at the shore. Clem tells Jimmy to play something else. Jimmy puts on a record by Louis Armstrong. I didn't hear its name. I'm sitting at the front of the boat writing my journal.

ℬ

Day 17 – Vienna

Vienna. We are worried by the lack of people on the streets. We have seen about ten people in the whole of Vienna. The shops are all closed and the doors are locked. We are told to meet our next contact in Der Burg Square. After ten minutes Clem says, 'I don't like this. Let's get moving, boys. He's either not coming or he's bringing company. And not the sort of company we want to meet.'

We all agree. It's not a case of being afraid, but our unit is now attached to our mission. Get home. Get home whatever it takes. Whether we have to drive across bridges, pull our automobiles out of rivers or across marsh or encourage strangers to aid our quest, we're all agreed that we must get to London.

It's not funny to realize the reality of our situation. We are now the rebels. We are now the ones out of our place. Rawalpindi is far away, in another time, in another country. There is no 1st or 2nd Battalion here to back us. We only have ourselves.

I think we were all truly lucky to get to Yaluva. I don't think Captain Afitap is insincere about helping us for a moment. Passing along the Danube as far as we have come has truly shown the mark of the man. Saints do not come close. If there is no place for the man in Turkey after the war, I'll find him one in Govan. I tell him that with a bit of help from Clem. The old man just smiles.

Captain Afitap deserves a medal and a treble. I learn that he does not drink whisky, either on the boat or off. We decide to drive around Vienna, to save us getting separated. Captain Afitap is also sending messages to London for us, through one of his neighbour's friends. The old man is not only bold, but as intelligent as Clem. We have all warmed to him and his only son, Kimsin.

&

Day 19

Salzburg Castle sits on the hill opposite our boat. We've sailed to the North of Austria. Coming as far as we can safely manage on our little Turkish boat, we know we must now disembark. We've already been stopped twice and searched. Using our Punjabi and Urdu, we ignore and confuse the sailors who stop us.

Captain Afitap is left to answer for us. He tells the sailors on both occasions to search the boat and assures them that they will find nothing. They shake their heads and leave us alone. The last boarding was just after we left Vienna. It made us uncomfortable. Not that we were scared. We had the guns, but no access to them. The questions lasted ten minutes before they were happy that we were Indian tourists. They watched us sail away from them. Then, they were gone. As soon as they were out of sight, Clem decided that he would carry his handgun in his inside jacket pocket in future.

'Ah was runnin oot o Punjabi,' Micky laughs.

'Aye, me an aw,' Huw agrees.

Just beyond the bridge, we finally make contact with our missing friend from Vienna. He hails us from the shore. Our contact, Dieter has Austrian papers for us and insists that we no longer pretend to be Indian. We immediately remove the boot polish from our faces. I'm not convinced it was working anyway.

ॐ

Day 20

We come across a bridge of Roman design. Judging by the collapse of the thing, Huw reckons it was built then too. The wooden replacement is a bone of contention. Four of us reckon it's safe to cross, two of us don't. Thankfully, rank is on our side. Otherwise I reckon we'd be heading back to Istanbul.

The question is, will the bridge take one automobile, never mind two? The boys decide the best thing to do is to examine the timbers and then to test the bridge very carefully. Angus is for none of that nonsense. He is the tall one, built like a stone latrine. He convinces Clem, Micky and Jimmy to bounce up and down on the bridge. 'If it can tak that,' Angus says, 'it isnae gonnae kill ye.'

Thank God, Govan and the King, we made it! Angus earns himself a thousand rupees in the process of waging against Huw and myself plummeting to our harm crossing the bridge. My question is, 'What happens then, Angus?' I'm still waiting for an answer. Although, to be fair, I did only ask the question after I'd driven across the damn bridge. Clem checks the chest is level on the back seat of the automobile I'm driving. Onward we go, on our mission. Jimmy reminds me of the film, Where There's A Will.

At the last corner, we found ourselves less than half a mile from an entire regiment of the Hun. We turned around sharply. Seeing a farmer coming towards us, we enlist his help in avoiding them. He kindly leads us along a dirt track that runs parallel to the railway. Having left the road we have no way to navigate until he suggests we follow him to the next village. A decision is made as to where we go from here. Nuremberg. I would have laughed if I had not known that Clem was deadly serious when he told us.

ജ

Day 21

We can see the ruins of a Castle on a hill nearby. We are not lost. We decide to avoid a one-sided gun battle, with yet another regiment of German Infantry. Angus is all for going at it himself until Clem insists we need to stick together. Having noted the railway earlier, we decide to wait until the Huns pass. We might even catch the next train. However, we soon realize even with planks, we will not be able to get on board.

After waiting for twenty minutes, we push on for two hours, keen to put as much distance between us and any German regiments. We are more alert to the daily dangers we now face. Micky says he would prefer to be out in the desert again, instead of hiding behind hedgerows. Jimmy agrees.

ℬ

Day 22

We have a bad feeling about entering Germany. Clem does not like the thought of entering the heart of Nazi territory. Angus looks like a bulldog chewing a wasp. Huw and Jimmy are worried that the big man will give us away. Jimmy and I are more concerned about the fact that Clem's uncle did not get his message through to Berlin. We're both Masons too. Micky says nothing.

It's no problem if Angus starts shouting, we'll silence him. However, if we are unable to reach London and fail in our mission, we will not be able to join the rest of our Battalion. That's important to all of us—to rejoin the other boys. Not only that, we have the chest. We have never discussed what we will do with it if we're captured. Having helped Clem to lift it into the tent on a nightly basis, I know that no one man could carry it while running.

It's just too heavy. It could possibly be buried and then retrieved. But then what?

৪৩

Day 23

We are almost into Germany. The mountains ahead are covered in snow. Unless we clear the road ahead of boulders, we will not make Nuremberg by noon tomorrow. Although we are on the border of Germany, at times, I feel as if we are back at the start of our journey. The landscape looks just as hostile. I know these mountains will outlive all of us. It is a very sobering thought.

We slept in luxury last night. We decided to stay in a hotel in twin rooms. I heard Jimmy and Huw talking until 2 a.m. Clem and I could hear Angus and Micky arguing over football teams. It felt good to be able to just lie in a bed and not bother about anything, like roads, chests or Nazis.

৪৩

Day 24

I awoke stiff this morning. My legs and my back ache. I tripped over the chest. However, after a quick breakfast we drove off. I think it might take me a week to get comfortable sleeping in a real bed again.

Even in the remote villages of Nazi Germany, we find wild propaganda against others. In front of me is a poster on a board—it is anti-Arab. On the left of the poster a German soldier is reading from *Mein Kampf* and the Arab is reading from the Qur'an. The message in the middle portrays all Arabs as evil. We know from our journey that no statement could be further from the truth. Jimmy asks me who thinks these things up. My response is, 'Some begger stuck in an office wha husnae travelled further than the tearoom.' Angus says, 'Ye ken lad Ah think yer mebbe richt. Ah dinnae hae onie worries til we sterted o'er thae hills back there. But noo, Ah really dinnae believe whit Ah'm seein here an am here seein it.'

Like many of the villages we have been through, this one has a handful of clearly recognizable buildings and features. Even without being able to read German, I can understand some of the posters and the places we should avoid being seen.

ॐ

Day 25

Thank God, Govan and the King! We have reached Nuremberg. Clem says that this is where it all started years ago. I've learnt that he is well-read and highly educated. He got a First at Cambridge. He only has three loves; hunting, reading and shooting. He talks about shooting with Micky, if they have time together. Clem admires the fact that Micky always has a steady hand. In the middle of the desert, Micky took out three rebels on his own. That seems so long ago now.

Our trip is nearly at an end. Nobody wants to discuss England. We have all avoided talking about it. Clem has improved his Turkish from basic to fluent. At every opportunity he was asking Captain Afitap what something was in Turkish. Captain Afitap appeared to see him as another son. The two bonded well. Here in Nuremberg, Captain Afitap and Rawalpindi seem like distant worlds.

We are hiding in plain view. Clem is of the opinion that standing in the middle of Nazi territory with our British automobiles and clothes is actually the safest place to hide.

It reminded me of how Charlie used to hide his money from 'Big' Maggie. He knew she had a fear of electricity. So, he would unscrew the light switch at Granny Fitzgerald's and hide six pence or a tuppence behind the wires. Even if my mother had found his money, she would never have got it herself. She'd tell him to give it to her. He never did. She'd then tell one of us to get it for her. We'd all run out the house saying we feared her, but we'd not be playing about with the electric, whatever she threatened us with. Granny Fitzgerald would just laugh and say, 'Whit monkeys they boys ur.'

ಬ

What a wonderful sight! Roads of cobbles. Sometimes on the dirt tracks we wish for cobbles, but on the cobbles you feel every bump. Clem is not happy when we have to stop. He is anxious to get to London, but does not say so.

We have to change the rear left tyre as it has worn through at the rim. It takes some time to move the new tyre into position. At least now, we know we will have a hot bath tonight. We have booked into a quiet little hotel nearby. We have been very careful not to advertise our presence here. The closer we get to the middle of Germany, the less comfortable we are. I have come across tigers and elephants on different patrols in the past, but this trip is above all those dangers.

We drive in a straight line at twenty miles per hour. By starting early in the day, we avoid driving at the hottest time. This is something we learnt from our desert drive. It is no fun to sit in hot seats for any length of time, even with the wind blowing in through the open canvas.

୫

Day 26

I wake to find we're stuck. The lead automobile is bogged down in a track. I cannot write road, as we have very rarely been on roads for days. Cattle and dirt tracks have really tested us all.

The metal in my arm means that I am unable to help the boys dig the automobile out. I lift a spade and muck in for half an hour. My arm is bleeding under my shirt. I'm in agony now. Angus and Clem

67

sit me on the wall after stealing my spade from me. Clem shakes his head. Jimmy says, 'Listen, wee man. Ye dinnae huv tae kill yersel on ma account. An as fur these other beggars? Ah'm no sae sure they want ye oot o it either. Sae dae us aw a favour an sit here a while. Me and Angus will huv her oot in a bit. Dinnae fret aboot the boys thinkin yer no daein yer bit. Ah'll shut the beggar up who says otherwise.' I just look at the blood coming from the wound beneath my shirt. I take a handkerchief and wipe the blood. My grimace is witnessed by Clem. He says, 'Right. You're off driving for a week, Jackie.' I'm about to argue the point, when Jimmy spins round. I just nod my head in acceptance.

ଓ

Day 27

Strong winds during the night. I thought I'd wake up in the Alps. Luckily enough, it died down after 5 a.m. I've been thinking and the only thing we have not seen on this journey is a blazing fire. We have seen rain, snow and floods, but no raging fires. Although, the heat of the sun in the desert after midday was close.

We are heading West. Our little convoy receives strange looks wherever we go.

I know why people stare. 'LONDON' is visible on the side of the automobile. I suggest to Clem that we might cover the words until we reach

England. He has already told Jimmy and Micky to cover a door each as soon as we stop tonight. We change tyres. The rim on the rear left tyre of the front vehicle is worn thin.

ℬ

Day 28

In order to reach London quicker, we decide to sail up the Rhine. Like so many other ships, we pass the Heinrich Kayser without incident. Although, we are watched closely by the crew. She's moving slowly and her wake does not throw us from side to side, unlike a cruiser we passed near Vienna. We negotiate a safe passage from Strasbourg to Cologne. Then we must drive to Paris. The six of us agree that it is too risky to sail all the way to London from Strasbourg.

French troops by the roadside convince us that we are indeed at war. We are getting closer and closer to the action. Occasionally, in the distance we hear thunder. We all know it is no natural force, but the guns of the enemy.

Sneaking across Germany reminded me of the time when my brother Robert ran through the close of Tam Wilson on his way home from school. Now, Tam worked nightshift like my father. And did his wife Eta not let rip at our Robert? She pinned Robert against the wall and cuffed his ear. Well, he came home whimpering. Never a good start with 'Big' Maggie. She asked him what he was whimpering for and got a slap for waking Tam Wilson. But, Eta Wilson got one hell of a shock when 'Big' Maggie pounded on her door. I was there. I followed my mother across the road.

'If ye touch onie o ma weans again, ye stupid bitch, I'll kill ye masel.'

'But, he woke oor Tam, Maggie,' Eta replied.

'Aye, and Ah dealt wi it. He'll no dae that again in a hurry. Ye keep yer hauns tae yersel.'

'Ah'm sorry, but Tam needs his sleep.'

'Aye, Ah ken, Eta. An Ah'm wantin ma weans fit tae work.'

'Just tell them to stay oot o the close then, Maggie.'

'Whit fur? They ur too scaert o me to cum onie where near here noo, Eta. But mind yer hauns, hen. They gie ye onie trouble an send fur me. Ah'll soon stop aw their nonsense.'

At this 'Big' Maggie loosened her grip from Eta's shoulders and our neighbour fell from the wall to the ground. After that we all became really good at moving up that close quietly. Well, our mates, Dougie MacLeod and Archie Clark lived on the top landing.

Before we set up camp for the night, Micky, Huw and Jimmy wash their clothes with Ajax on a wooden bench. Ajax is actually for cleaning floors. It's at least a way of getting the dirt out of our clothes. This is the only way to combat stinking like a month old chop. We try to wash ourselves in rivers whenever we can. It's not as nice or relaxing as sitting in a hot bath, but we have to do it. We maintain our personal grooming routines as we did in India. I cannot wait to visit a barber.

§

Day 29

Paris. At last. No meetings. Clem sends a telegraph to London. A quick lunch and then we are off again. After a long and heated conversation, I drive the next leg. Clem is glad of a break.

Jimmy is in the back seat wondering what shows might be on in London. He says he fancies a slap-up meal and taking a young lady dancing and to the shows. I think he's already spent his next month's wages before he has even earned them. He knows exactly what he wants. He's very focused and I think that's an admirable quality in anyone.

Micky, Angus and Huw are in the other car. We can see them arguing about who is driving next. It's funny to watch. One nods his head and the other two shake. Another nods his head and the other two shake. One points left and another right. It reminds Jimmy, 'of Laurel and Hardy and Buster Keating.' I'm not sure who is Buster Keating and who is Stan Laurel, but I know Angus is supposed to be Oliver Hardy.

§

Having telegraphed London from Paris that we are in urgent need of supplies, we are somewhat amazed when a gentleman in a tweed jacket hails us. His name is Godfrey Braithwaite. He is a Reverend of the Anglican Church of England.

Angus asks, 'Bloody hell, Clem did ye tell em we were starvin oot 'ere?'

'No, I merely said we needed supplies, Angus.'

'Supplies, ye say. Well, we've got a bloody piss bucket each. And whit the hell are we wantin wi cushions, water jugs an lamps. Is somebody takin the . . .'

'Maybe they don't want us to starve, Angus.' Clem replies.

'Richt. That'll be it. Noo we're nigh but at the back door, the beggers think mebbe they should gee us a wee bit o a hand. Christ almighty, Clem.'

'No, it's the Reverend Godfrey Braithwaite, Angus.' Clem concludes the conversation in order that we should not be caught unawares.

Three hours later, we sail from La Harve. It's a rushed job and we nearly lose the black automobile into the English Channel. We still have it, due to the fact that Jimmy swung out on a loose chain and collided heavily with the rear side of the vehicle. He hurt his shoulder, but didn't say to anyone until we were an hour from shore.

ꙮ

Almost home. The crew of the H.M.S. Adamant want a closer examination of our boat. We wait for them to board us before we admit that we're British. Our papers confirm our story. They marvel at the fact that we have driven from India. Well, mostly. We insist they do not give us an escort, in order to maintain our disguise as a Finnish cargo ship.

We're less likely to be sunk by the enemy if we're seen as a neutral party.

After communicating with the Captain of the Adamant, the boarding party leave us. Nothing is said that would alert onlookers. We all stare at the boarding party's clean uniforms. The Officer-in-Charge informs us that he will communicate his findings in full to his Captain when he re-boards the submarine supply ship. He shakes his head when he looks at the state of our clothes. It is only then that we realize they're nothing now but torn rags.

As we move along the coast, we can almost touch England with our bare hands. It's good to know that in a few short hours, we will be back on hard ground. British soil. We will be able to finish our mission and deliver the unopened chest. Clouds are looming above us. It's strange to think that we did not experience rain in the deserts.

Clem asks if I want to meet his uncle at the Temple Lodge. 'Aye, that'd be great, Clem,' I say.

❧

Coming across a private sailing boat is a great sign. Clem gives an audible sigh of relief. We wave to the Captain of the vessel and his companion. We are so close to London. Jimmy is tapping his foot and Micky looks ready to dive in and swim to shore. Angus says nothing, but stands aft considering something invisible. Huw is smoking a cigarette. We know that even now we are a target.

'We're like twa ducks on a pond,' Huw says.

'Quack. Quack,' Jimmy replies.

Moments later, we realize the harsh reality of life in Great Britain. Our first thoughts are that Herr Hitler is going to stop us. The Warship that passes is British and we all breathe a sigh of relief. It does not stop us, but sails slowly past. Several crew members aboard the ship view us from the aft of the vessel. Its wake disturbs our little craft, even at such a great distance. For a moment we hold the guard rails and ropes until the sea is calm again.

∞

Day 30

Our arrival prompts more questions than it does celebrations. The dockyard workers ask us if we really did drive all the way from India. Angus asks if they can read. Four of them say they can. Angus says, 'Well, if ye're aw certain o that ye'll no go asking onie mair stupid questions then, will ye?' The blank expressions on their faces and the looks among them, convince the rest of our unit that both the speed of Angus's response and the reply itself, failed to be understood. Huw looks at Clem. Clem nods. Huw replies, 'Us 2nd Battalion boys can do it twice as quick as onie other lot. We're goin aff tae London noo. There we ur gonnae huv the best pints of oor lives. You boys can cum wi us, if ye want tae?'

At this the foreman, from Paisley, insists that his gang return to their duties. Two hours later, we are on the road to London.

&

The morning is rather misty and cold in London. We are all thrilled to be driving along the banks of the Thames. Angus and Huw have exchanged money. Angus reckoned we'd reach HQ before noon. Huw was quite certain we'd all drown in the English Channel. It is a rather cold and horrible morning. The weather is in stark contrast to the heat we left in India. Although we are wet, we are a happy bunch. We are home. God Save the King!

We are drunk on happiness. Our bodies ache and we cannot imagine the welcome we will get. We are not concerned about how HQ respond to us. Our problems are over. Whatever happens now, we are back on British soil. A sight, Micky now admits, he doubted he would ever see again. Jimmy just stands with an open mouth. Angus shrugs his shoulders. I'm just hoping I can find my brother Charlie in this large city.

Captain Afitap, before we left him and his son, Kimsin, said we were champions of men and the bravest he has ever seen. He shook our hands with a tight grip. Captain Afitap said Clem's as honest as an anchor chain is long. We did not know why he said that or why he had a tear in his eye at our leaving. I will never know.

I'm looking forward to a cooked breakfast with bacon, eggs and a potato scone. Both my uniforms and my two changes of civilian clothing are well worn. I must get new shoes too. Both pairs have holes in them. Later, if I have time I'll ask where to get new ones.

Big Ben and Parliament. What great sights! We are on the south shore of the Thames. Our legs are stiff and even though we've had food enough and a change, we know we've unfinished business. Nobody has seen Clem. He has disappeared. He has left us a note to meet him at the Ministry. Jimmy says he heard Clem slip out rather than eat with the rest of us. Whatever is in that chest he was carrying to the cab, with the help of the driver, must be important. Clem has never let it out of his sight. He always slept beside it. I doubt I will ever know the answer as to what it contained, but it must have been incredibly valuable and of great benefit to King and country for us to put ourselves through the perils we've faced as a unit.

Epilogue

I'm sitting in the White Hall Inn, Edinburgh. It is 2 p.m. We all agreed to meet here on 1st November after the war ended. When the one o'clock gun sounded, I was excited at the thought of seeing the boys again. The sound of that gun took me back to my billet here in Edinburgh and to the faces of Campbell and many more.

I knew Angus wouldn't meet me here. He was with me at Dunkirk. I'll never forget the look of horror on his face, when an enemy shell passed straight through his chest. One minute we were running for the boats, the next I was diving, but he was too slow. It had only been a split second. The look of confusion in those eyes. The look of pain. The look of utter disbelief. It lingers even now.

Jimmy ran back onto the beach for the wounded again and again. After the 8th return, he was too tired to make it back onto the boat without help. All the lads he had rescued gave him a huge cheer. (I returned twice, my arm bleeding through my uniform. Both times, I had been trying to get to Angus. I never reached him.) Jimmy later died on his return to France, during the final push to Berlin.

Huw was killed in Egypt in '42 by a mine, during the push into Libya. I was going to tell the others, but not of the deaths I have seen, just the reasons why some of the boys would not be coming. Men of battle do not do that—discuss death. As for Micky?

I have no idea. In Holland we separated into different units. I've not seen him since.

The barman tells me this is the oldest pub in Edinburgh. He also tells me that it is the most haunted. I'm quite certain it does have some spirits, but more of the medicinal kind. As I walk to a table he informs me (reliably or not) that Robert Burns once stayed here.

Do I have a hero? Is there any one man greater than them all for me? The beaches, fields and deserts are covered with the footfalls of so many unknown heroes. Men, who gave their all in some small personal battle, rising to face the onslaught of an enemy. Often outgunned and outmaneuvered, it was only the heroes unfaltering bravery that outclassed their enemies. I cannot say exactly when I decided that I respected Clem most of all. Not in any way was it a sudden decision. It was more a case of realizing what I had known all along on the impossible journey.

At 3.30 p.m. a young woman enters the pub. She walks up to me and asks,

'Jackie?'

'Yes,' I reply.

'I'm Jessica,' she continues, 'we met in India a long time ago.'

'I remember.'

She hands me a letter and waits for me to speak. I know the writing. It's from Clem. The letter reads:

Well boys,

Where are we now? If you are reading this, I'm dead. You can sell my Ford for me, Jimmy. I'm one of the lucky few. I escaped from the camps on three occasions. I was convinced THEY would shoot me. THEY never did. I always thought THEY had someone feeding them our landing points in France. Only time will tell, boys. Only time will tell. Sorry to say, Micky was killed in Normandy. Tell Huw I know I still owe him four shillings and tuppence and that he can get it from the sale of the automobile.

I guess there are too many blanks left, boys. In solitary, I'd often think of our long trip across half the world and the generosity of the strangers we met. I can only thank you brave few who dared to believe we could do it. And we did it, boys. We actually did it. Thanks to each of you, the chest survived the impossible journey.

I'll never forget Captain Afitap, nor Angus's face when we all arrived in Nuremberg. The Big Man was always unstoppable even then. Not lost for words, I can still see his dry mouth as he said, 'Well, mebbe noo they'll gee us aw a drink in wan o' they Beergartens.' So, Angus have a beer on me pal. And leave one for me too . . . just in case . . . if any beggar touches it, I'm sure you will deal with them, Big Man. Happy trails, boys!

Best,

Clem.

&

I thank Jessica and give her fifty pounds for Clem's Ford. I seem to have an attachment to that vehicle like Clem had for the chest. I hand her the Talisman that Clem wore and she drops the Fords keys on the table. The chain is broken.

She stops suddenly as if about to say something else, but then after a pause, merely coughs. She stands there, motionless in time like the faces I have seen and caught on camera. But times have moved on. Jessica has moved on too, judging by her protruding belly under her half open raincoat. She has a new life.

After she disappears through the door onto the street, I buy the boys a drink. I keep thinking that they may be stuck in a military hospital, but know that is not the reality of the war—our war. I still expect one of the boys to come through the door even now. Yet, I know I am the sole survivor.

I'm sitting on my own at a table with five full beers untouched. For a moment, I see their faces and hear their laughter at the table as I had when we were at our clubs in Lahore, Delhi and Calcutta. I'll be leaving for Glasgow in twenty minutes time and I know as soon as my first footfall touches the pavement outside that all the drinks will disappear. The barman was right about their being ghosts in here, after all.

My Demob suit is wearing thin at the elbows. My trousers are patched at the knee. I have no intention of returning home for more than a short visit to see my father and brothers. Then, I'm thinking of going for a long drive.

PICTORIAL NOTES

The following photographs are only a sample of the extensive collection that was taken by my late great uncle, John Coghlan, during his time in India and beyond. Since my undergraduate degree, I have been fascinated by India and the multicultural aspects of its society.

I felt that the work of the unsung heroes in India and beyond during the 1930' and 40's should be celebrated. To this end, I detailed the rescue of British soldiers by the Indian Army. I believe that the soldiers of the British Army were often in more danger from the elements in the far reaches of the Commonwealth than from any one person. The photographs in this novella hopefully capture that point.

I find it remarkable that anyone could have driven from Rawalpindi to London during the 1930's.

James A. Coghlan
Alloway, 2008

Markhor, Abdulla and their sons

Entertainment on the trip

Digging our way out of another problem

Boarding the boat in Yaluva

The Blue Mosque, Istanbul

Another moment of courage in Europe

Taking the quiet road to London

The Canal in Nuremberg

Arriving back in Great Britain

ENGLISH TRANSLATIONS
OF
SCOTTISH DIALECT

Page 11

'Bugger off then and get yourself killed, you selfish little bastard.'

.   .   .   .   .   .

'You are an ungrateful little bastard.'

.   .   .   .   .   .

'She will have calmed down a bit by then.'

.   .   .   .   .   .

'Remember not to get yourself killed, Jackie. And say goodbye to the old man. You know he will miss you too.'

Page 11-12

I replied, 'I will write to you once I am billeted. I will write to Granny Fitzgerald.'
'Make sure you do that, Jackie. You need to know how Rangers are playing.'
'I will. See you, Charlie. And make sure you do tell me.'
'I will have your winter jacket.'
'Fine.'
'And I will also have your. . .'

Page 12

'I will miss you Jackie, lad. But, I will not stop you.'

Page 13

The RSM only said, 'You have made your bed, Rifleman. Get on with it.'

Page 15

Campbell says, 'I am not going for your throat, Coghlan. I am going to kill your jam sandwich.

Because every one knows people from Glasgow cannot do without their sandwich.'

I laugh, 'Yes, well, it is better than being a butter boy.'

'Butter boy?'

'Yes, one of those boys who slip up.'

Page 20

When Campbell is about to leave Black asks, 'Did you enjoy the biscuits as much as the tea, Campbell?'

'No, bit too dry for me, sir.'

'Well, that'll be an end to the matter, Rifleman. No repeats, I hope.'

'With those biscuits? No chance of that sir.'

Page 21

As usual, Charlie ends the letter, 'Take care of yourself, Jackie.'

Page 24-25

She often said, 'Good for nothing that one.'

Page 27-28

'You boys are lucky to be riding home,' Corporal Chisholm says as I step into the 2nd automobile.

'Are we?,' I reply.

'Yes, freedom and the open air. Not stuck in a tin can out at sea.'

'You are right about that,' I reply.

'Wish I was going. Got any room?'

'No. Not this time, Corporal.'

Page 30

Angus says, in his rather humorous tone, 'Then the buggers cannot say you've been at it, Jackie. If they think you've been on your arse the whole trip, you'll end up behind a desk lad. I'm not for it myself.'

.   .   .   .   .   .

I'm a bit suspicious of it all, but then as they say, 'You can take the man out of Govan, but you cannot take Govan out the man.'

Page 31

I reply, 'I'm just glad we're on our way again. I thought or a minute we might have to go back.'

Page 39

'It's a box full of hope. Hope that must reach London. Whatever it takes.'
'Ok, Clem. I was only asking.'
'And I'm only telling.'
'Let me see.'
'I'm not allowed to do that. The chest cannot be opened.'
'Why not?'
'Just listen to me. Forget it's even here. Just forget it.'

Page 41

And where I am from, you use one or both to outrun the police through the tenements.

.   .   .   .   .   .

Angus says, 'Listen to me lad, if you think I am going to run away you can. . . . Orders is orders, sir.'

Page 45

Micky says, 'I do not mind the quiet, Jackie. I just cannot stand all the sand in my food.'

Page 49

After Clem shows us all the telegram, Angus asks, 'What do that lot think we're all doing? Shooting bloody rabbits? Did you not tell them Clem?'

Page 53

I say, 'As a lad I would sit with him or go on a walk down the quay.'

I overhear Angus saying, 'The little man will cover our backs, I tell you that.'

Page 54

'It's great. The Hun would never think of it. Six Scots disguised as Indians, on a Turkish boat, sailing the Danube,' Micky shakes his head as he repeats what Clem tells us.

Page 55

'Well, little man, you'll not have to do the graveyard shift tonight,' Micky says.

Page 57

Angus and I hear Jimmy say, 'You might not want to say too much Scots there boys.'

Page 61

'I was beginning to run out of Punjabi,' Micky laughs. 'Yes, me too.' Huw agrees.

. . . . . .

'If it can take that,' Angus says, 'It will not kill you.'

Page 65
My response is, 'Some beggar stuck in an office who has not travelled further than the tearoom.' Angus says, 'You know lad I think you're maybe right. I did not have any worries until we started over they hills back there. But now, I really do not believe what I'm seeing here and I'm here seeing it.'

Page 66
Granny Fitzgerald would just laugh and say, 'What monkeys they boys are.'

Page 68
Jimmy says, 'Listen, little man. You do not have to kill yourself on my account. And as for these other beggars? I'm not so sure they want you out of it either. So do us all a favour and sit here a while. Me and Angus will have her out in a bit. Do not fret about the boys thinking your not doing your bit. I'll shut the beggar up who says otherwise.'

Page 70
'If you touch any of my children again, you stupid bitch, I'll kill you myself.'
'But, he woke our Tam, Maggie,' Eta replied.
'Yes, and I dealt with it. He'll not do that again in a hurry. You keep your hands to yourself.'
'I'm sorry, but Tam needs his sleep.'
'Yes, I know, Eta. And I'm wanting my children fit to work.'

'Just tell them to stay out of the entry then, Maggie.'
'What for? They are too scared of me to come any where near here now, Eta. But mind your hands, dear. They give you any trouble and send for me. I'll soon stop all their nonsense.'

Page 72
Angus asks, 'Bloody hell, Clem did you tell them we were starving out here?'
'No, I merely said we needed supplies, Angus.'
'Supplies, you say. Well, we've got a bloody piss bucket each. And what the hell are we wanting with cushions, water jugs and lamps. Is somebody taking the . . .'
'Maybe they don't want us to starve, Angus.' Clem replies.
'Right. That'll be it. Now we're almost at the back door, the beggars think maybe they should give us a little bit of a hand. Christ almighty, Clem.'

Page 73
'Yes, that'd be great, Clem.' I say.

Page 74
'We're like two ducks on a pond,' Huw says.

.   .   .   .   .   .

Angus says, 'Well, if you are all certain of that you'll not go asking any more stupid questions then, will you?'

.   .   .   .   .   .

Huw replies, 'Us 2nd Battalion boys can do it twice as quick as any other lot. We're going off to London now. There we are going to have the best pints of our lives. You boys can come with us, if you want to?'